G000038338

# Where There's a Will There's a Relative

### by

## Roger Karshner

SAMUEL FRENCH

FOUNDED 1830

NEW YORK HOLLYWOOD LONDON TORONTO

SAMUELFRENCH.COM

Copyright © 2008 by Roger Karshner

ALL RIGHTS RESERVED

CAUTION: Professionals and amateurs are hereby warned that *WHERE THERE'S A WILL THERE'S A RELATIVE* is subject to a royalty. It is fully protected under the copyright laws of the United States of America, the British Commonwealth, including Canada, and all other countries of the Copyright Union. All rights, including professional, amateur, motion picture, recitation, lecturing, public reading, radio broadcasting, television and the rights of translation into foreign languages are strictly reserved. In its present form the play is dedicated to the reading public only.

The amateur live stage performance rights to *WHERE THERE'S A WILL THERE'S A RELATIVE* are controlled exclusively by Samuel French, Inc., and royalty arrangements and licenses must be secured well in advance of presentation. PLEASE NOTE that amateur royalty fees are set upon application in accordance with your producing circumstances. When applying for a royalty quotation and license please give us the number of performances intended, dates of production, your seating capacity and admission fee. Royalties are payable one week before the opening performance of the play to Samuel French, Inc., at 45 W. 25th Street, New York, NY 10010.

Royalty of the required amount must be paid whether the play is presented for charity or gain and whether or not admission is charged.

Stock royalty quoted upon application to Samuel French, Inc.

For all other rights than those stipulated above, apply to: Samuel French, Inc., at 45 W. 25th Street, New York, NY 10010.

Particular emphasis is laid on the question of amateur or professional readings, permission and terms for which must be secured in writing from Samuel French, Inc.

Copying from this book in whole or in part is strictly forbidden by law, and the right of performance is not transferable.

Whenever the play is produced the following notice must appear on all programs, printing and advertising for the play: "Produced by special arrangement with Samuel French, Inc."

Due authorship credit must be given on all programs, printing and advertising for the play.

ISBN 978-0-573-66393-2          Printed in U.S.A.          #25283

No one shall commit or authorize any act or omission by which the copyright of, or the right to copyright, this play may be impaired.

No one shall make any changes in this play for the purpose of production.

Publication of this play does not imply availability for performance. Both amateurs and professionals considering a production are strongly advised in their own interests to apply to Samuel French, Inc., for written permission before starting rehearsals, advertising, or booking a theatre.

No part of this book may be reproduced, stored in a retrieval system, or transmitted in any form, by any means, now known or yet to be invented, including mechanical, electronic, photocopying, recording, videotaping, or otherwise, without the prior written permission of the publisher.

## IMPORTANT BILLING AND CREDIT
## REQUIREMENTS

All producers of *WHERE THERE'S A WILL THERE'S A RELATIVE must* give credit to the Author of the Play in all programs distributed in connection with performances of the Play, and in all instances in which the title of the Play appears for the purposes of advertising, publicizing or otherwise exploiting the Play and/or a production. The name of the Author *must* appear on a separate line on which no other name appears, immediately following the title and *must* appear in size of type not less than fifty percent of the size of the title type.

# ACT ONE

## Scene One

*(**PLACE:** Sam Price's townhouse.)*

*(**SETTING:** The set consists of a living room stage left and bedroom stage right. The rooms are separated by a partition and are connected by a door. There is a hallway left, off the living room, leading to the entrance. Regarding the living room: it contains a couch, chairs, TV, coffee and end tables, a large chest, an armoire, a desk, a fireplace with a mantle holding a clock, and wall-shelves stocked with books. There is a telephone on one of the end tables. A large picture window overlooks the city. As to the bedroom: there is a large bed, nightstands, a cabinet, a chest of drawers, and a desk with a chair. In the wall, right, is a door leading to a guest bedroom, and there is a closet door downstage right.)*

*(**AT RISE:** Sam Price's relatives are gathered in the living room. There are **ZELDA**, Sam's sister; **RUDY**, Zelda's son; **JERRY**, Sam's brother; **SALLY**, Jerry's daughter. In the dimly-lit bedroom we can barely discern Sam's "body" in a four-poster bed with gossamer side curtains. A mannequin represents the body.)*

**ZELDA.** *(on the couch, wiping her eyes with a Kleenex)* What a terrible thing, Jerry.

**JERRY.** He was a wonderful brother to both of us.

**SALLY.** *(in a chair)* Yes...a wonderful person.

**JERRY.** *(standing next to the armoire)* And so generous. After Esther and I divorced, he let me stay in his spare bedroom.

**ZELDA.** The man was a saint.

**RUDY.** *(pacing)* He was always thinking of others.

**ZELDA.** *(in a chair)* Yes, and the perfect gentlemen. He stood back. He opened doors.

**RUDY.** I'll never forget the time he posted my bail.

**ZELDA.** *(drinking from a bottle of water)* You weren't at fault, Rudy; the other driver should have sensed you were drunk.

**SALLY.** There'll never be another like him.

**JERRY.** They threw away the mold, Zelda.

**ZELDA.** This is largely true, Jerry.

**RUDY.** *(looking out of the window)* And look at the way he lived. Nobody would know he was loaded.

**SALLY.** With all of his money he still wore a Timex.

**JERRY.** He owned one suit.

**ZELDA.** The man was humble, and he became a deeply religious Catholic person.

**RUDY.** The time I went with him to church, he put a hundred bucks in the collection basket. And he didn't ask for change. *(sits on the couch next to his mother)*

**ZELDA.** I've never understood their religion. Up and down, up and down, never in their seats.

**RUDY.** I couldn't have asked for a better uncle, Mom.

**ZELDA.** Or me a better brother. When we were kids he'd always give me the first lick of his ice cream.

**JERRY.** When Sally was in the hospital he came and told doctor jokes. Isn't that right, honey?

**SALLY.** He had the pathologist in stitches.

**JERRY.** The man never had a bad word for anyone.

**ZELDA.** Such a loss.

**SALLY.** As they say, Aunt Zelda, the good ones die too early.

**ZELDA.** As they say.

**RUDY.** He used to take me on his lap and read me the business section.

**JERRY.** When my bike was stolen, he let me ride his.

**ZELDA.** *(rises and paces)* There were many kindnesses.

**RUDY.** *(standing at the fireplace)* Even though he didn't like dogs, he never kicked one.

**ZELDA.** Sam was the perfect brother, Jerry. Always there when we needed him.

**JERRY.** This I can't deny.

**SALLY.** He loved the outdoors.

**ZELDA.** Especially the park.

**RUDY.** He always carried a pocketful of peanuts.

**JERRY.** *(takes a chair)* To feed the squirrels?

**RUDY.** No, he just liked peanuts.

**ZELDA.** *(crosses to and stands at the window)* I can't believe he's gone.

**SALLY.** *(leaves her chair and joins* **ZELDA** *at the window)* A person never knows. Here one day...

**JERRY.** He shoulda gone to the doctor sooner.

**ZELDA.** I tried to tell him.

**SALLY.** People tend to let things go.

**RUDY.** It all started with just a spot.

**ZELDA.** But he wouldn't leave it alone.

**SALLY.** He kept picking at it.

**RUDY.** This is what happens when you get too much sun.

**ZELDA.** He had a very fair skin that covered his entire body.

**JERRY.** It finally took over his leg.

**SALLY.** Don't remind me. I'm allergic to illness.

**RUDY.** *(leaves the fireplace and sits in a chair)* The surgeon said it was like operating on a bowl of walnuts.

**ZELDA.** Mother tried to warn him. But he wouldn't cover up.

**JERRY.** I wonder why he wanted to be laid out at home?

**ZELDA.** He had a phobia about funeral homes. It was his final request.

**RUDY.** He was a big man; we may have to get six-and-a-half pallbearers.

**SALLY.** After Louise died he went downhill.

**ZELDA.** He was never the same.

**SALLY.** Maybe his grief went to his leg.

**JERRY.** Too bad they never had kids. He woulda made a wonderful father.

**ZELDA.** They would have been a comfort after Louise passed. We're the only family the poor man had.

**RUDY.** I'm sure he appreciated us. When he was sick, I called him everyday.

**JERRY.** Sally called him twice. Didn't you dear?

**SALLY.** *(She rises and stands behind the couch.)* It was the least I could do, Dad.

**ZELDA.** *(Leaves the window and returns to the couch.)* Rudy would have called him more often but he didn't want to tire him out.

**RUDY.** Yeah, I was being considerate.

**JERRY.** I'm sure he took care of us in his will.

**ZELDA.** Who else? We're the next in line. But I never think about it. Whatever he left me will be appreciated.

**SALLY.** It's the last thing on my mind.

**JERRY.** Likewise.

**RUDY.** Maybe he left me the townhouse.

**SALLY.** Why you?

**RUDY.** I was his favorite.

**SALLY.** No, *I* was his favorite. If anyone deserves the town-house, it's me.

**RUDY.** What would you do with a townhouse, Sally?

**SALLY.** I'm a city person. I'd be close to shopping.

**RUDY.** I'm more of a city person than you'll ever be. Every-day I'm on the streets rubbing elbows.

**JERRY.** Now now, you two. Look…I'm sure we will all be well taken care of.

**ZELDA.** What about the very busy insurance business and the beach house with water that comes all the way up to the shore?

**RUDY.** Sally can have the beach house.

**SALLY.** I don't want the beach house. I don't know why Rudy needs the townhouse.

**RUDY.** I'm gonna need a place to live after I marry Doris Cappallini.

**ZELDA.** What!?

**SALLY.** Doris Cappallini!?

**ZELDA.** Forget it! No way! No son of mine's marrying the daughter of a crook.

**JERRY.** You're mother's right, Tony Cappallini's reputation is all over the city.

**SALLY.** We'll be a social disgrace. I'll have to cover up when I leave the house.

**ZELDA.** Rudy, I won't have you mixed up with a family like that. I've told you a thousand times, Tony Cappallini has Mafia written all over him.

**RUDY.** Doris and I are in love.

**JERRY.** Why can't you find a nice girl who's not a descendant of Al Capone?

**ZELDA.** You can forget about it. It's out of the question.

**RUDY.** You can't stop me.

**ZELDA.** You marry that person and I disown you. I'm cutting you off completely.

**RUDY.** You wouldn't.

**SALLY.** Can you blame her?

**JERRY.** Your poor uncle is probably turning over in his grave.

**RUDY.** He's not buried yet.

**JERRY.** It's a mercy he's dead. This way he won't have to be disgraced by a Cappallini.

**ZELDA.** If you marry that girl, whatever your uncle left you I'm contesting on the grounds you're insane. I'm not having you throw away my brother's hard earned money on some woman whose father is two steps away from the federal prison.

**RUDY.** But Mom…

**ZELDA.** No buts!

**RUDY.** *(stamping his foot petulantly)* You can't boss me around. I'm not a kid. I'm twenty-six going on twenty-seven.

**JERRY.** We have a reputation to uphold. I have an important business to think about.

**RUDY.** Important business? You're a calendar salesman.

**SALLY.** I don't know what in the world you see in Doris Cappallini.

**RUDY.** She's a beautiful girl with olive oil skin.

**SALLY.** I saw her picture in the papers when she was voted Ms. Salami. She still has big hair.

**JERRY.** You never know what you're getting into with these people. One minute they give you the shirt off their back, the next they strangle you with it.

**SALLY.** Last year they had Cappallini up on Tax evasion. Then his factory burns down. Next his business partner is found in a laundry bag in Jersey.

**RUDY.** Yeah, and they couldn't prove a thing.

**SALLY.** And oranges don't fall far from the tree.

**RUDY.** Apples.

**ZELDA.** What's wrong with that nice Cartwright girl I introduced you to?

**RUDY.** C'mon, Mom, she's old before her time.

**ZELDA.** She's only twenty-four.

**RUDY.** Yeah, and already she complains of arthritis. And she wears support hose. The lines in her forehead look like corduroy. This is normal?

**SALLY.** But she's from a good family.

**JERRY.** They own horses.

**ZELDA.** And her family will pay for a big expensive wedding. Black tie. The bridesmaids will be wearing custom made gowns.

**RUDY.** And the bride will be coming down the aisle on crutches. Forget about Sara Cartwright, I'm not marrying a young senior citizen.

**ZELDA.** I'm warning you, Rudy. You marry that girl...nothing. You'll get zilch, nada.

**RUDY.** I don't care, I'm marrying Doris Cappallini. She's a gorgeous woman.

**SALLY.** Now, yes, but after a few years she'll be fat and three inches shorter.

**JERRY.** And your kids will be a criminal element.

**RUDY.** What am I hearing here? Stereotypes. Prejudice. Thank God my poor dead uncle can't hear any of this. He loved everyone...even Greeks.

**ZELDA.** No wedding! The case is closed! I won't discuss it. I'm getting a serious headache.

**JERRY.** Besides, we have bigger matters here. We got a division of property to consider.

**ZELDA.** It all depends on the will.

**SALLY.** Have you ever read it?

**ZELDA.** No.

**JERRY.** Sam wouldn't discuss it.

**ZELDA.** It wasn't in his safe deposit box.

**JERRY.** Sam was a very private person.

**RUDY.** I think he had a lot of hidden cash.

**SALLY.** Really?

**JERRY.** What gives you this idea?

**RUDY.** Once, before we went to the park, he reached behind the clock and pulled out three thousand bucks.

**ZELDA.** No!

**RUDY.** I'm not kidding. *(going to the clock on the mantle)* Three thousand dollars...right here...behind this clock. *(reaching behind the clock, feeling about)* Ah, ha! *(He withdraws a bundle of bills and displays them.)* What about this?

**JERRY.** I'll be damned.

**SALLY.** Wow!

**ZELDA.** I don't believe it.

**RUDY.** *(flipping through the money)* Look at this.

**SALLY.** How much?

**RUDY.** I dunno. *(going to the coffee table)* Gimmie a minute.

*(He sits on the couch and sorts the money carefully on the coffee table, counting under his breath.)*

**ZELDA.** I knew Sam was close, but I didn't know he was a miser.

**JERRY.** He just didn't trust banks. Or the stock market.

**ZELDA.** He was heavy in real estate.

**JERRY.** No, he was heavy in slums. His tenants had rat bites.

**ZELDA.** You can't hold it against him for thinking smart, Jerry. He was ahead of the curve. A visionary.

**JERRY.** And they all paid cash. The man didn't know what a rent check looked like.

**SALLY.** He always had a roll of money on him. Once, at the circus, when he bought cotton candy, he tried to get the vendor to cash a thousand dollar bill.

**JERRY.** The man never owned a credit card.

**ZELDA.** He was careful.

**JERRY.** Face it, he was tight.

**ZELDA.** But he paid for Rudy and Sally's college.

**JERRY.** It was a loan. At ten percent. We're still paying it off.

**ZELDA.** But it was a kind gesture. Where would the kids be today without an education?

**JERRY.** Probably working, out making an honest living.

**RUDY.** *(counting out the last bill)* There…

**SALLY.** *(Bending over RUDY)* Well…how much?

**RUDY.** Five thousand. I'll leave it on the coffee table. We can split it up later.

**SALLY.** Fantastic!

**ZELDA.** Five thousand!

**JERRY.** Amazing.

**SALLY.** Imagine…this kind of money lying around.

**JERRY.** Undeclared.

**ZELDA.** Thank God he never had a fire.

**RUDY.** I think we're in the middle of a gold mine.

**SALLY.** You think?

**RUDY.** The place is probably crawling with bucks.

**JERRY.** Yeah. Dough's probably hidden all over the place. *(heading for the fireplace)* I'm checking the fireplace.

**SALLY.** *(heading for the armoire)* I'll check the armoire.

*(During this interlude, the players conduct a searching frenzy.* **JERRY** *goes to the fireplace and digs about in its flue.* **SALLY** *opens the armoire and rummages through its contents.* **ZELDA** *begins to remove books and look behind them.* **RUDY** *looks under the couch cushions, into the chest. They make random comments as they search: "Nothing here," "Nothing," "Nuts," "It must be somewhere," "I wonder where he put it," "Where in the hell?" etc. The search is carried to extreme, under carpets, under furniture.* **ZELDA** *and* **RUDY** *begin to search the deceased's bedroom as* **JERRY** *and* **SALLY** *continue their quest in the living room.)*

**RUDY.** *(looking under* **SAM**'s *mattress)* I feel like I'm robbing the dead.

**ZELDA.** Don't worry dear; he'd want us to have it.

**RUDY.** Maybe there's a secret panel.

**ZELDA.** He was funny about money. When he paid the bill, he'd never let you see how much he tipped. What if Jerry and Sally find it first? Can we trust them?

**RUDY.** Are you kidding? You heard what Sally said about the townhouse.

**ZELDA.** My own flesh and blood. Keep looking. *(they continue their search of the bedroom)*

**SALLY.** *(removing books and looking behind them)* I wonder if there's a secret panel?

**JERRY.** *(moving the couch)* Or a trap door.

**SALLY.** Five thousand is just the tip of the iceberg.

**RUDY.** *(going to the closet)* I'll check the closet. Maybe he stuffed it in his shoes. *(He enters the closet.)*

**JERRY.** *(looking under the couch)* What if they get to it first? You think they'll tell us?

**SALLY.** You saw how Rudy jumped on the townhouse.

**JERRY.** We have to keep and eye on 'em.

**ZELDA.** *(looking under the bed)* Find anything, dear?

**RUDY.** *(offstage, from the closet)* No.

**ZELDA.** Nothing? What about the pockets of his suit?

**RUDY.** *(leaving the closet)* He's wearing it. And I'm not searching the body. It's disrespectful. *(entering the spare bedroom, right)* I'll look in the spare bedroom.

**ZELDA.** *(probing)* Good idea.

**RUDY.** *(offstage, in the spare bedroom.)* I wonder what Uncle Jerry and Sally are up to?

**ZELDA.** I wonder.

**RUDY.** *(offstage)* Where there's money involved, you can't be too careful, people will resort to anything.

**ZELDA.** They even steal United Way cans.

**SALLY.** I never realized how greedy Rudy was.

**JERRY.** My own nephew, who I've known since a baby, circling like a vulture.

**SALLY.** He's been around the Cappalinnis too much.

**JERRY.** Being too close to relatives doesn't pay. Especially when it comes to dollars and cents.

**SALLY.** Sometimes you're better off with complete strangers. With relatives you always feel obligated to pick up the check.

**ZELDA.** Find anything, dear?

**RUDY.** *(coming from the spare bedroom)* Nothing.

**SALLY.** I think we'd better see what they're up to.

**JERRY.** Good idea.

**ZELDA.** I wonder what's going on in the living room?

**RUDY.** I dunno, but I don't trust them. We'd better check.

> *(ZELDA and RUDY head for the living room as JERRY and SALLY head for the bedroom. When RUDY opens the bedroom door the couples meet face to face in the doorway in an embarrassing encounter.)*

**ZELDA & JERRY.** Find anything?

**SALLY.** No.

**RUDY.** No.

**ZELDA.** Are you sure? Maybe you didn't look so good.

**SALLY.** We looked high and low.

**JERRY.** Up and down. What about you in the bedroom?

**ZELDA.** Likewise. High and low.

**RUDY.** Up and down.

**SALLY.** Just in case, I think we'd better take a look for ourselves.

**ZELDA.** You don't trust us?

**JERRY.** Of course, Zelda, of course. But, as they say, another pair of eyes...

**ZELDA.** As they say.

**RUDY.** In that case, Mom and I will take another look in the living room. Just in case.

**SALLY.** Just in case.

**RUDY.** Forget about the spare bedroom, it's nothing but spare.

*(They switch sides, ZELDA and RUDY into the living room, JERRY and SALLY the bedroom. They begin to search the rooms again.)*

**SALLY.** *(at the bed, looking under the mattress, noting Sam's body)* He looks so peaceful. There's a smile on his lips.

**JERRY.** *(digging through the closet)* That's because he's surrounded by money.

**ZELDA.** *(rummaging)* They had guilt written all over their faces.

**RUDY.** *(scrounging)* In neon letters.

**SALLY.** *(digging)* I think they know something.

**JERRY.** *(snooping)* I could tell Zelda was covering up. I've seen that sneaky smile a million times.

*(The couples continue to search.)*

**SALLY.** You could sense they were uneasy.

**JERRY.** My own flesh and blood.

**RUDY.** I think they know more than they're letting on.

**ZELDA.** I can see right through Jerry. Since we were kids. He had the same look as when he used to steal the Monopoly money. My own brother.

**RUDY.** Families are a mixed blessing.

**ZELDA.** You never know.

**SALLY.** You see how fast they wanted to get into the living room? They don't trust us.

**JERRY.** My own sister. Who can a person trust?

**SALLY.** Already Rudy wants real estate.

**JERRY.** To move into with a bimbo.

**ZELDA.** Not trusting his own sister. And I'm the first one to buy a calendar every January.

**SALLY.** I never realized I had a greedy cousin.

**RUDY.** Did you see how big Sally's eyes got when she saw the five thousand?

**ZELDA.** Why do you think she called Sam twice a day? She was angling.

**JERRY.** A person who would marry a Cappallini…who knows? Already he's got mob tendencies.

**RUDY.** What if they've already found the money?

**SALLY.** What if they've found the money?

**ZELDA & JERRY.** Where would they hide it?

**SALLY.** It's probably on them.

**RUDY.** I could be in Jerry's coat pocket.

**JERRY.** They've found it. I'll bet on it.

**SALLY.** I'll bet it's in Rudy's jacket. I noticed a bulge.

**ZELDA.** This is the reason they were acting so sheepish.

**JERRY.** We'll split up the five thousand and they'll leave with a fortune. But they're not gonna get away with it.

**RUDY.** We can't let 'em get away with it. Let's get in the living room.

(**RUDY** and **ZELDA** *make a beeline for the bedroom as* **JERRY** *and* **SALLY** *head for the living room. Again they meet as the bedroom door is opened. They register shock.*)

Oh! *(embarrassed laugh)* We were just coming in to help out.

**JERRY.** Us, too.

**SALLY.** Yes, we figured eight eyes are better than four.

**ZELDA.** *(chuckling nervously)* As they say.

(**JERRY** and **SALLY** *step into the living room.*)

**JERRY.** Any luck?

**ZELDA.** No. You?

**SALLY.** Nothing.

**RUDY.** I can't understand it.

**JERRY.** *(approaching* **RUDY***)* Rudy...look at you.

**RUDY.** What?

**JERRY.** Are you losing weight?

**RUDY.** Not that I know of.

**JERRY.** You look thinner.

**RUDY.** That's funny.

**JERRY.** What?

**RUDY.** I was just thinking the same thing. You look thinner, too. Doesn't he, Mom?

**ZELDA.** A regular reed.

**JERRY.** *(throwing his arms around* **RUDY***)* Let me look at you.

**RUDY.** *(throwing his arms around* **JERRY***)* Me too.

*(The men begin to pat each other up and down.)*

**JERRY.** *(patting)* You've dropped a ton.

**RUDY.** *(patting)* You too. How'd you do it?

**JERRY.** *(patting)* I went on the Scarsdale. How about you?

**RUDY.** *(patting)* I cut back on the starches and trans-fats.

**JERRY.** *(patting)* Amazing. There's nothing to you.

**RUDY.** *(patting)* I'm feeling a bone rack.

*(The men part, each satisfied that the other is not carrying cash.)*

Well, whatever you did, you look like a million.

**JERRY.** Likewise. You look twenty years younger.

**RUDY.** I'm only twenty-six, Jerry.

**ZELDA.** It's generic. When our father, rest his soul, was forty, he had to show his ID to buy beer.

**SALLY.** Apparently the only money was behind the clock.

**ZELDA.** So it seems.

**JERRY.** But what the hell did he do with the slum money?

**RUDY.** He probably had it laundered.

**JERRY.** Damn!

**SALLY.** Let's look on the bright side. Each of us is twelve-fifty to the good.

**ZELDA.** Chump change.

**SALLY.** It's probably all tied up in the estate.

**JERRY.** Let's hope he avoided probate.

**ZELDA.** Let's hope.

*(The telephone rings.)*

**RUDY.** Now what?

**ZELDA.** *(going to the phone)* It's probably the undertaker.

**SALLY.** He gives me the creeps. Can you imagine where his hands have been?

**ZELDA.** *(answering)* Hello...oh, yes... *(covering the receiver, addressing the group)* It's Father Michaels. *(back on the telephone)* Yes, Father Michaels?...The will?...No, I have no idea...Yes...What!? He did what!? *(pause as she listens)* I don't believe it! I mean, he couldn't have, I mean... You did? She did?...Yes, I know he was very religious, but...Really?...I don't know anything about it...Yes, of course I'll look...Yes...Good-bye.

*(She hangs up. She is ashen, obviously shaken.)*

Holy Jesus!

**RUDY.** What?

**SALLY.** What is it?

**JERRY.** What's going on?

**ZELDA.** *(slumping to the couch)* Father Michaels claims Sam left everything to the church.

**SALLY.** No!

**RUDY.** He couldn't!

**ZELDA.** I can't believe it.

**RUDY.** I don't buy it.

**ZELDA.** Michaels says he saw the will.

**SALLY.** So what? So he said he saw the will. It's our word against his.

**ZELDA.** He says he has a nurse as a witness.

**RUDY.** That's bad. Witnesses are bad. Why would Sam do something like this?

**JERRY.** Face it, the man was an eccentric…one suit, money behind the clock.

**ZELDA.** Yes. He was a wonderful man, but unconventional.

**SALLY.** He seemed to be preoccupied a lot.

**RUDY.** *(He begins to pace.)* He got things mixed up.

**SALLY.** He never could figure out which one of us was which. Half the time he called me Rudy.

**ZELDA.** *(She rises and begins to pace.)* Especially in his final days.

**JERRY.** I think the melanoma went to his head.

**ZELDA.** God only knows what he promised Father Michaels.

**JERRY.** *(He rises and begins to pace.)* He was delirious. He didn't know where he was.

**ZELDA.** Right before he died he took my hand and asked me for directions to Staten Island.

**RUDY.** The poor man didn't know what he was doing.

**JERRY.** Down the drain…millions of dollars, real estate, a big insurance business – all going to the church. Damn!

**SALLY.** *(She rises and begins to pace.)* As if they need it.

*(The others rise and pace with nervous anxiety, up and down, back and forth, crisscrossing.)*

**ZELDA.** They don't even pay taxes.

**RUDY.** They'll probably invest in another fast-food chain.

**ZELDA.** I understand they're heavy in Denny's.

**JERRY.** The poor won't see a penny of it, you can bet on that.

*(They converge, bumping into one another centerstage.)*

**RUDY.** This is crazy, we gotta calm down.

**ZELDA.** Yes, we have to keep our heads.

**JERRY.** Right, panic proves nothing.

*(They all sit. A brief silence.)*

**JERRY.** What do you know about this Michaels character?

**ZELDA.** He took over St. Catherine's after Father O'Connor retired. The first time I met him was when he came to the hospital after Sam lapsed.

**RUDY.** They love the lapse.

**SALLY.** They have a way of showing up at death's door.

**ZELDA.** They're like bloodhounds. They gotta nose for the nearly deceased.

**JERRY.** I don't know about you, but the last thing I wanna see when I come out of a coma is some guy in a black suit standing over me with a cross.

**ZELDA.** He seemed very personable.

**JERRY.** Of course. Personable is their thing.

**ZELDA.** He was alone with Sam when I showed up.

**SALLY.** That says it all. He got Sam to promise him everything. He preyed on a dying man.

**JERRY.** He wore him down with fear.

**RUDY.** Just think, I was on the verge of a townhouse.

**JERRY.** And I would have taken over the insurance business.

**ZELDA.** Who says he was going to leave you the business?

**JERRY.** We discussed it.

**ZELDA.** I was under the impression he was going to leave the business to Rudy.

**SALLY.** The townhouse *and* the insurance business?

**JERRY.** Why would he go and leave a successful business to a kid?

**RUDY.** Because I got fresh ideas.

**SALLY.** Name one.

**RUDY.** Drive-through insurance offices.

**JERRY.** What!? The business would go down the toilet.

**SALLY.** I was under the impression he was going to leave me money to open a chain of body-waxing salons.

**RUDY.** How'd you get that idea?

**SALLY.** We talked.

**ZELDA.** How come conversations were going on behind my back?

**JERRY.** Things came up. Like they seem to have with Rudy running the insurance business.

**ZELDA.** Rudy was his favorite.

**JERRY.** Over his own brother?

**SALLY.** *I* was his favorite.

**RUDY.** Since when?

**SALLY.** Since he told me in the hospital.

**ZELDA.** I thought you said you couldn't stand hospitals because hospitals make you nervous.

**RUDY.** She was angling for the body waxing.

**JERRY.** Sally wouldn't do such a thing. She doesn't need his money; she has a future in cosmetology.

**ZELDA.** Four years of college loans for facials.

**SALLY.** You were with him more than anyone during his final days. How do we know you didn't con him out of everything?

**ZELDA.** I didn't have conversations, I had compassion. I was there when they drew blood, when they gave shots. After they brought him home from the hospital who was with him when they gave him his last rites in Latin? I was always closest. When he had his double hernia, who drove him to his operation? When Louise died, who went with him to pick out a reasonably priced casket?

**RUDY.** This is going nowhere. We don't know what Sam wanted till we find the will.

**JERRY.** But nobody can locate the damned thing. It wasn't at the bank.

**ZELDA.** Then it has to be here.

**SALLY.** You think?

**JERRY.** Where else?

**RUDY.** If he hid money, why not his will?

**JERRY.** You gotta point. But where?

**RUDY.** The key to our future is right here in this townhouse.

**SALLY.** Yes.

**JERRY.** *(jumping up)* Well then…let's get looking.

> *(They go into a searching frenzy, moving furniture, pulling up rugs, looking under objects, digging through the armoire, probing every nook and cranny. Books are torn from their shelves and thrown to the floor, things are overturned. They work their way to the bedroom. They race about with wild abandon, commenting as they pillage.)*

**RUDY.** Why wouldn't he give it to a lawyer like a normal person?

**SALLY.** Because he wasn't normal.

**JERRY.** Rich people are eccentric.

**ZELDA.** You think he would have thought about his relatives.

**JERRY.** His wonderful brother and sister.

**RUDY.** And his nephew.

**SALLY.** And niece.

**ZELDA.** A person should always tie up loose ends.

**JERRY.** When it came to business, he was careful.

**ZELDA.** But with personal stuff he was sloppy.

**RUDY.** Where the hell would he put it?

**SALLY.** Keep looking.

**JERRY.** Maybe we'll come across the money.

**ZELDA.** We should have insisted that he write everything down.

**RUDY.** When it came to money, he clamed up.

**SALLY.** Maybe it's plastered up in the walls.

**ZELDA.** He wouldn't go to that extreme.

**SALLY.** Let's hope the will's legible.

**ZELDA.** I can't imagine where he put it.

**SALLY.** It couldn't just up and fly away.

**JERRY.** That damned priest.

**ZELDA.** I don't trust him. He's constantly checking the stock market on his cell-phone.

**JERRY.** These people are up to their catechisms in money.

**RUDY.** And they cry poor.

**SALLY.** Think what they'd get if they'd ever sell the Vatican.

**ZELDA.** They're very shrewd business people.

**JERRY.** In Jesuit school they spend more time on economics then on religion.

**RUDY.** I understand they may make a takeover bid for the Mormons.

**JERRY.** Find anything?

**SALLY.** Nothing.

**ZELDA.** Where in the world…?

**JERRY.** Did the man ever dust?

**ZELDA.** He hasn't cleaned since Louise. This is what happens when men live alone.

**RUDY.** I give up.

**SALLY.** Don't give up. Keep looking.

**RUDY.** This is a waste of time.

**JERRY.** It's bound to turn up.

*(They are searching every inch of the bedroom.)*

**SALLY.** What about the body?

**RUDY.** What about it?

**SALLY.** It may be in his suit.

**RUDY.** If it is, it'll have to stay there.

**ZELDA.** Why would it be in his suit?

**JERRY.** Why not? We've looked everywhere else.

**RUDY.** Forget it.

**JERRY.** How can you forget millions of dollars?

**ZELDA.** Jerry has a very good point.

**SALLY.** I'd do it, but I'm allergic to dead people.

**RUDY.** I'm not touching the man.

**SALLY.** Your townhouse may be in his pocket.

**JERRY.** And my insurance business.

**ZELDA.** I think he'd want us to look.

**RUDY.** You do?

**SALLY.** Certainly.

**JERRY.** Of course. *(pointing to* **RUDY***)* And you're the obvious choice.

**RUDY.** Me!? Why me?

**SALLY.** I thought you said you were his favorite.

**RUDY.** You said you were.

**SALLY.** I was, but I can't even shake hands with the undertaker.

**JERRY.** *(with his arm around* **RUDY***'s shoulder)* Millions, Rudy.

**RUDY.** Hey! What about you?

**JERRY.** I think it should be you. I'm being polite.

**RUDY.** Oh yeah, sure.

**SALLY.** You were his only nephew.

**RUDY.** I'm not searching a dead man.

**ZELDA.** He won't know anything about it.

**JERRY.** Tellya what, I'll flip you for it. Okay?

**RUDY.** Are you nuts?

**JERRY.** *(reaching into his pocket and withdrawing a quarter)* Heads or tails?

**RUDY.** I don't trust you.

**JERRY.** I'll let it fall on the carpet.

**ZELDA.** This is fair, Rudy.

**RUDY.** You're all crazy.

**ZELDA.** Think about your inheritance.

**JERRY.** Call it!

**RUDY.** I dunno…

**SALLY.** Call it, Rudy.

**ZELDA.** Fifty-fifty are good odds, honey.

**RUDY.** *(Reluctant)* Well…Okay…Heads!

> *(JERRY flips the coin and it tumbles to the carpet. Everybody surveys the result.)*

**JERRY.** Tails!

**RUDY.** Damn!

**ZELDA.** Don't worry dear, he won't bite you.

**RUDY.** *(moving toward the bed)* This is sick.

**JERRY.** Millions, Rudy, millions. *(Picks up the quarter.)*

**RUDY.** Okay, okay, all right! Jesus!

> *(He goes to the bed, pulls back the curtain, and reaches in.)*

**SALLY.** Be sure to check his pockets good.

**RUDY.** *(groping)* I'm checking, I'm checking.

> *(The others anxiously stand by as he searches.)*

**SALLY.** *(breaking the silence)* Well…?

**ZELDA.** Find anything, dear?

**RUDY.** Yeah.

**SALLY.** You did!?

**RUDY.** *(withdrawing from the curtains and straightening them)* Yeah…lint.

**JERRY.** Nuts!

**ZELDA.** Nothing?

**RUDY.** Nothing.

**SALLY.** Then where is it?

**JERRY.** We've practically vacuumed the place.

**RUDY.** *(picking up a magazine from the nightstand)* Look at this.

**SALLY.** *(approaching)* What is it?

**RUDY.** A girlie magazine. It was part of his junk we brought home from the hospital.

**ZELDA.** It couldn't be Sam's. He wasn't like that. He couldn't stand nudity. He even wore socks in the sauna.

**JERRY.** But a man has needs.

**RUDY.** *(Flipping through the magazine.)* It's hard to imagine that he would read such... *(A paper falls from the magazine and flutters to the floor.)*

**ZELDA.** What's that?

**RUDY.** *(picking up the paper)* I dunno.

**SALLY.** Do you think maybe...?

**JERRY.** Could it be...?

**RUDY.** *(scrutinizing the paper)* It's the will!

*(They all gather around* **RUDY.***)*

**ZELDA.** The will. I'll be damned.

**JERRY.** Fantastic!

**SALLY.** The last place anyone would look for it. Pressed between smut.

**ZELDA.** Well...what's it say?

**JERRY.** Yeah, c'mon, what's it say?

**RUDY.** *(squinting at the paper)* Gimmie a minute, okay? It's hand-written, I can't make it out.

**ZELDA.** *(grabbing the document from* **RUDY***)* Gimme that. *(looking at the paper)* It's Sam's writing all right.

**RUDY.** So?

**SALLY.** So, what's it say?

**ZELDA.** I'm looking, I'm looking.

**JERRY.** So look faster.

*(There is a pregnant pause as* **ZELDA** *scans the document.)*

**RUDY.** Okay, so what's the story?

**ZELDA.** *(lowering the paper with an air of dejection)* He left it all to the church.

*(A pall falls over the scene. They leave the bedroom, enter the disheveled living room, and fall into the chairs and couch. There is a long, depressing silence.)*

**JERRY.** Screwed.

**RUDY.** Yes.

**SALLY.** This is very depressing.

**ZELDA.** As they say, you never know.

**SALLY.** As they say.

**RUDY.** How can you figure such things? It goes to show you can't depend on anything.

**JERRY.** Not when there's money involved.

**ZELDA.** *(rising with a air of resignation)* Well…we can't do a damned thing about it.

**RUDY.** There must be something.

**ZELDA.** What we can do is straighten the place up before people show up to view the remains.

**SALLY.** I don't know if I'll be able to greet them. I'm too depressed. I feel like somebody just died.

**ZELDA.** *(going to the bookshelves)* C'mon, we gotta get this place back together.

**JERRY.** *(rising)* Yeah

(**RUDY, JERRY** and **SALLY** *begin to replace things, straighten the furniture and rugs, close drawers, pick up scattered objects in both the living and bedroom.* **ZELDA** *returns the books to the shelves.)*

**ZELDA.** It's a sad thing when a rich blood relative doesn't remember his wonderful family. *(noting a book before placing it on a shelf)* Look here, the Holy Bible.

**RUDY.** We'd all be better off if he hadn't read it.

**JERRY.** If the man had stayed an atheist, we'd all be rolling in dough. But, oh no, he has to go and get religion after Louise passes.

**ZELDA.** I think it was guilt for not letting her have a new kitchen.

**SALLY.** One of us should have been at the hospital twenty-four-seven. This way Michaels couldn't have gotten to him.

**JERRY.** Sneaky bastard.

**RUDY.** I don't know how we missed him.

**JERRY.** Maybe he dropped the goofy outfit, came in disguised as a normal person.

**ZELDA.** A priest would stoop to that?

**JERRY.** They stoop, they stoop.

**SALLY.** Especially when they stand to inherit enough to buy another casino.

**ZELDA.** And he promised to take care of us.

**RUDY.** This is the reward I get for being a decent nephew. When he was sick I spent every Monday morning with him.

**SALLY.** I spent every Wednesday right after my nail appointment.

**RUDY.** He didn't appreciate what a special family he had.

**ZELDA.** It breaks my heart to think about it.

**JERRY.** You think you know someone, but...

**ZELDA.** You never do. Even your own brother.

**RUDY.** I don't think he had any idea how much we loved him.

**SALLY.** As if any of us were expecting to get anything.

**JERRY.** We were only there to support him.

**ZELDA.** There was nothing we wouldn't do. I stopped by the hospital every day with magazines.

**RUDY.** Too bad they weren't Penthouse.

**SALLY.** I hate to say it, but I think the man was a deeply religious pervert.

**ZELDA.** I'll never believe that magazine was his. Even though he cut us out of our inheritance, Sam had pure thoughts.

**SALLY.** I guess I can forget about the body waxing business.

**RUDY.** Thank God it won't make any difference to the Cappallinis.

**ZELDA.** What about Cappallinis?

**RUDY.** They're gonna pay for the wedding.

**ZELDA.** What wedding? No wedding! What are you, hard of hearing for a young person? You marry that Italian and I don't know you.

**RUDY.** They're making plans.

**ZELDA.** Behind my back my own son's planning his wedding

to a Sicilian. If you father was alive he'd have a fatal heart attack.

RUDY. They're not Sicilian, they're Calabrese.

ZELDA. What's the difference?

JERRY. My shoe repairman was a Calabrese. He cheated me on heels.

SALLY. I'm not attending such a wedding. I'm not having my picture taken with gangsters.

JERRY. Who's gonna be your best man... Al Pacino?

SALLY. They'll probably be wearing shoulder holsters under their tuxes.

ZELDA. You'll never have my blessing as long as I'm breathing.

RUDY. You don't know anything about these people.

JERRY. I also had an Italian gardener. He went off on the ride mower...I'm haven't seen him since.

RUDY. These are very generous people.

JERRY. But they expect something in return.

TONY. Mr. Cappallini treats me like a son.

ZELDA. No wedding!

RUDY. Quit telling me what to do.

ZELDA. That's it! Enough with Cappallinis, the case is closed. We have bigger things to think about. We have to figure out a way of getting around the church.

JERRY. You're mother's right, we can't let 'em get away with this.

SALLY. I think we should confront Father Michaels.

RUDY. What good would that do?

SALLY. Maybe we can shame him into giving us back the estate.

RUDY. Shame? What shame? These people have no shame. Even the bingos are fixed.

SALLY. What if we brought it up at the funeral, in front of everyone? Maybe we could embarrass him into giving it back.

**JERRY.** Embarrass? You kidding? You could run it on the Internet.

**ZELDA.** What we need is a good lawyer. I'll call Irv Goldstone.

**JERRY.** That crook?

**ZELDA.** He gets results. The man's a regular tiger. He'll sue the cassocks off 'em.

**SALLY.** It would be all over the papers that we're suing a religion. How would we look? You don't go around suing God.

**ZELDA.** What would God know?

*(They continue straightenng.)*

**RUDY.** What we need is a scheme.

**JERRY.** Yeah.

**ZELDA.** Schemes aren't easy, they take a crafty mind.

**JERRY.** I'm crafty.

**ZELDA.** No you're not. People see through you like looking at X-rays. Scheming isn't you.

**RUDY.** Wait a minute! What are we worrying about? We don't have a problem.

**SALLY.** Of course we have a problem.

**RUDY.** No we don't. All we gotta do is tear up the will. Who will know?

**JERRY.** He's right! No will, no proof.

**ZELDA.** Forget it.

**SALLY.** It's perfect.

**ZELDA.** It's not so perfect. Michaels has a nurse as a witness. Remember?

**JERRY.** So what? It's their word against ours.

**ZELDA.** Our word against a nurse and a priest?

**RUDY.** We're finished.

**SALLY.** So we bribe the nurse. They're all underpaid for emptying bedpans.

**ZELDA.** This could be risky.

**SALLY.** As they say, nothing ventured…

**ZELDA.** As they say.

**RUDY.** Forget it. We can't go around bribing nurses.

**JERRY.** Rudy's right, it's not a clean plan.

**SALLY.** What we need is a diabolical mind.

**JERRY.** It's too bad Ralph Sizemore's in prison, he always had great ideas.

**RUDY.** It's not easy being shifty. You gotta have experience.

**ZELDA.** Even though crooks are a problem, you gotta hand it to them for imagination.

**SALLY.** There must be an angle.

**JERRY.** We don't need an angle, we need a miracle.

**RUDY.** *(dropping what he's doing, an epiphany)* Hey! Wait a minute! I got it! That's it!

**SALLY.** What's it?

**RUDY.** Tony Cappallini!

### End of Act One

# ACT TWO

## Scene One

*(One hour later.)*

*(The rooms have been put in order; money gone from the coffee table. The family alternately sits, stands and crosses. There is a palpable atmosphere of anxiety.)*

**SALLY.** It's a stupid idea.

**RUDY.** You got a better one?

**SALLY.** No, but…

**RUDY.** Well…?

**JERRY.** I don't like it.

**ZELDA.** You think I like it? Being in the same room with a Cappallini? But we have to be practical.

**RUDY.** From my point of view, the man couldn't be nicer.

**JERRY.** Thank God there won't be children present.

**ZELDA.** Sometimes you have to make a pact with the devil.

**SALLY.** I hope he doesn't bring his big-hair daughter.

**RUDY.** The man's savvy. He has answers. He gets things done. He has friends.

**JERRY.** How do you define "friends?"

**ZELDA.** Look, if he can get around the church I'm closing my ears. I hear nothing.

**RUDY.** He's a charming man. And a thinker. He has good taste and a complete Sinatra record collection. You should see his house.

**SALLY.** I've seen it. It's way too big for the lot.

**RUDY.** The man paints on a big canvass.

**JERRY.** I'm only going along with this for the family and because I think Michaels is a bigger crook than Cappallini.

SALLY. I'm allergic. I hope he's not wearing that heavy Italian cologne.

RUDY. Look, before he gets here we all have to agree to show the man respect. These people are big on respect.

JERRY. I'm not kissing any rings.

RUDY. That's crazy. Where do you get these ideas?

JERRY. You think I live with my head in the sand? All you have to do is read the papers, watch the late news. Look at the oil prices.

RUDY. What's oil have to do with it?

JERRY. Wise up. These people are behind OPEC.

SALLY. I didn't know that.

ZELDA. No kidding?

JERRY. The government's in on it, and so is the Pope.

RUDY. I'm related to crazy people. And you're concerned about Cappallini? At least he isn't nuts.

SALLY. I'm not shaking his hand.

ZELDA. Hey! Against my better judgment, I'm bending over backwards here so we won't lose millions. If I can bend over backwards, you and Sally can at least lean a little bit. Is it too much to ask?

JERRY. Okay, maybe I'm willing to bend. But not over backwards.

SALLY. I can bend slightly, but only for a couple of hours.

JERRY. As a special favor to my wonderful sister, who I know in her heart would rather sleep with snakes than deal with weasels, I'm prepared to bend.

RUDY. Good. *(The doorbell sounds.)* There he is now. *(heading for the entrance hall.)* Now remember...respect.

*(He disappears into the entrance hall. His voice offstage.)*

Tony! Welcome.

**TONY.** *(offstage)* Hi ya, kid.

(**RUDY** *enters from the entrance hall followed by* **TONY CAPPALLINI**. **TONY** *is handsome and the archetypical gangster: slick black hair, expensive black suit, a black shirt with a white necktie, glossy black leather shoes. He exudes brash self-confidence and is suave and relaxed in contrast to a family riddled with angst. A large pinkie ring is on the little finger of his right hand. He is toying with a large, unlit cigar, from time to time placing it in his mouth.* **RUDY** *makes introductions and salutations are exchanged.)*

**ZELDA.** Sit down, Mr. Cappallini.

**TONY.** Tony.

**ZELDA.** Tony. Have a seat. So nice of you to come at a time like this with a dead person in the bedroom.

**TONY.** *(patting* **RUDY***'s cheek affectionately)* Anything for Rudy. He's a beautiful boy. *(Sitting in a chair. The family also sits.)* He reminds me of my late partner, Vito Nuccio, rest his soul.

**JERRY.** I read about it. How could a man drown in the Mojave Desert?

**TONY.** They had a very wet year.

**SALLY.** *(laying it on)* How is your beautiful family?

**TONY.** The family's good. Thank God. *(crossing himself with his cigar)*

**JERRY.** How's business?

**TONY.** Things could be better. We currently have a lot of receivables. So...I understand you folks gotta problem.

**JERRY.** It's got to do with Sam's will.

**TONY.** *(motioning in the direction of the bedroom)* Sam being the dead individual in the bedroom.

**RUDY.** He was my uncle.

**ZELDA.** The poor man fell victim to a melanoma that took over his entire person.

**SALLY.** And he was loaded.

**TONY.** So?

**RUDY.** He went and left everything to the Catholic Church.

**JERRY.** He got conned.

**ZELDA.** The priest got to him while he was in a weakened state.

**SALLY.** He didn't know what he was doing because he was distracted. He was thinking of heaven.

**TONY.** Which priest?

**RUDY.** Father Michaels at St. Catherine's.

**TONY.** Ah ha…that guy.

**JERRY.** You know him?

**TONY.** Yeah, he shorts the unions on lawn fetes. A very unattractive habit.

**JERRY.** See, I told you he was a crook.

**ZELDA.** He says he saw the will and he has a nurse as witness.

**TONY.** Witnessness ain't good.

**ZELDA.** His poor loving family will be getting zilch while the church buys more condos.

**RUDY.** It isn't right.

**TONY.** Right ain't got nothing to do with it.

**JERRY.** Can you help us?

**TONY.** I dunno.

**SALLY.** Rudy says you know angles.

**TONY.** Maybe.

**ZELDA.** By the way, what kind of business are you in, Mr. Cappallini?

**TONY.** The collection business. We cover the entire East Side. We used to cover the entire city but we had a little dispute with certain parties who were very unreasonable.

**JERRY.** This happens. Even in the calendar business.

**SALLY.** I recently saw a picture of your daughter in the Times.

**TONY.** Doris. I'm blessed.

**SALLY.** A beautiful girl.

**TONY.** She takes after the Tellaricos on my wife's side. All good-looking people from Sicily. Her Grandfather Gino had his hair in his nineties. He was a tailor. Made a nice suit. *(indicating* **RUDY** *with his cigar.)* The kid here and Doris should have beautiful children.

**ZELDA.** This is something we have to discuss.

**TONY.** What's to discuss? They have my blessing.

**ZELDA.** I think we should talk in private.

**TONY.** Private? What's private? Aren't we all friends here?

**RUDY.** What's to discuss? My mind's made up.

**ZELDA.** You stay outta this. Mr. Cappallini…

**TONY.** Tony.

**ZELDA.** Tony, we have to talk. In private.

**TONY.** Okay, if you insist.

**RUDY.** This is ridiculous.

**ZELDA.** We can talk in the bedroom.

*(***ZELDA*** rises and moves to the bedroom door, followed by* **TONY**. *They enter the bedroom. The lights dim in the living room and the remainder of the family sits in tableau.* **TONY** *notes* **SAM***'s body.)*

**TONY.** Just like the old country, having the body at home. It brings back memories.

**ZELDA.** Sam was funny about dying.

**TONY.** There ain't nothing funny about dying. Dying is a serious business because it's very permanent.

**ZELDA.** He hated funeral homes.

**TONY.** What's to like? Even though many of my dear business acquaintances became members of the funeral of the month club, I've never got used to 'em.

**ZELDA.** Tony…about Rudy and Doris…

**TONY.** They're gonna make a beautiful couple.

**ZELDA.** I think maybe it's not such a good idea.

**TONY.** What are you talkin' about? They're perfect. You should see 'em together.

ZELDA. Rudy's too young. He hasn't lived.

TONY. What? The kid's a man.

ZELDA. He isn't ready for a family. He doesn't even have a job.

TONY. No problem, I'll put him in the collection business. I'll give him Queens. My last guy had an unfortunate occurrence.

ZELDA. You don't realize, he's very immature. He wouldn't know what to do with a baby. He might drop it.

TONY. The kid's old enough to make up his own mind. Besides, I made plans. It'll be the biggest wedding of the year. The Food Services Union is catering the whole thing for nothing. I got good friends in the AFM; we'll have the best musicians for no bread. We'll be getting a million dollar wedding for only a hundred grand.

ZELDA. It sounds wonderful, Tony, but I can't give my blessing.

TONY. What!? No blessing? What am I hearing here?

ZELDA. I know I can't stop him, but I can't give my blessing.

TONY. I'm being honest, Zelda, I beginning to take this as a personal offense. And I come here in good faith, willing to help you out of a jackpot.

ZELDA. And I appreciate it.

TONY. And I'm hearing that a wedding made in heaven won't have your blessing. Why should I be helping a person with no blessing? Besides, how do you know I can help?

ZELDA. Rudy says you know angles.

TONY. This may be, but I' not giving angles for no blessing.

ZELDA. It's nothing personal.

TONY. No blessing and it's nothing personal? With no blessing, I don't help.

ZELDA. It's up to you.

**TONY.** Why should I be helping people who are insulting the name of Cappallini? My daughter, the Garlic Queen, isn't good enough?

**ZELDA.** I'm sure she's a lovely person. For a nice Italian boy. It would be an ill-fated marriage. They're from two different worlds. And Rudy can't eat spicy food.

**TONY.** If this is the case, I'm respectfully declining to assist with your personal problem.

**ZELDA.** It would be a nice thing for Rudy to be getting an inheritance. I thought you liked the boy.

**TONY.** Like him? I love him like son.

**ZELDA.** Then why not a little consideration? Why let a personal problem get in the way?

**TONY.** It's a matter of respect.

**ZELDA.** I have respect. You're a smart man. I could tell that the minute you walked in with your suit.

**TONY.** I appreciate that.

**ZELDA.** Tony, I'm asking you to help Rudy. He could inherit a townhouse. A townhouse has substantial market value.

**TONY.** Without a blessing I should be bending in all directions?

**ZELDA.** You said you loved him like a son.

**TONY.** The kid is beautiful.

**ZELDA.** Then do it for him.

**TONY.** It goes against my better judgment to be helping people who give no respect.

**ZELDA.** Isn't it better that we get what's rightfully ours rather than having it go to a priest who cheats the unions?

**TONY.** I gotta admit, I hate to see anything go Michaels. He refused to christen my niece, Maria, after my long-time associate, Jimmy the Plummer, unfortunately perished by falling on a kitchen knife.

**ZELDA.** Then do it for Rudy.

**TONY.** I hate to weaken on this issue.

**ZELDA.** Look at it as a humanitarian gesture. You'll be helping a beautiful boy.

**TONY.** Well…

**ZELDA.** And, at the same time, you'll be sticking it to a crooked religious person.

**TONY.** If I decide to help, it's gotta be my way. Understand?

**ZELDA.** Of course.

**TONY.** No interference.

**ZELDA.** None.

**TONY.** For Rudy.

**ZELDA.** I'll be grateful till the day I no longer breathe on this earth.

**TONY.** *(after a thoughtful pause)* All right. But this is a big concession.

**ZELDA.** I understand.

**TONY.** Okay, then, let's get to angles.

*(Lights up on the living room as* **TONY** *and* **ZELDA** *return from the bedroom.)*

Okay, let's try to figure this thing out.

**ZELDA.** When I think of my dear dead brother in there being taken advantage of…

**JERRY.** By someone with too much starch in his collar. Who the hell do you trust in this world anymore?

**TONY.** *(taking a seat)* Trusting is for chumps.

**SALLY.** Any ideas?

**TONY.** I'm thinking, I'm thinking.

**RUDY.** Don't rush the man while he's thinking.

*(There is a long pause as* **TONY** *falls into deep concentration.)*

**JERRY.** Can't you think faster?

**TONY.** I'm thinking as fast as I can, okay?

**ZELDA.** Rudy says if there's a way out you'll find it, that you can figure out anything.

**TONY.** It depends. This is a different situation. I usually have business acquaintances take care of problems. Now don't bother me.

*(a long silence as* **TONY** *thinks)*

**SALLY.** Anything yet?

**JERRY.** Relax, can't you see the man is concentrating?

**RUDY.** I wouldn't be surprised if Michaels has already gotten lawyers.

**ZELDA.** A team of Jesuits. They train for this kind of thing.

**TONY.** I'm getting an idea.

**SALLY.** He's getting an idea.

**TONY.** Okay. All right! I think I got it!

**JERRY.** You hear that? He thinks he's got it.

**RUDY.** Have you got it?

**TONY.** Yeah.

**SALLY.** What have you got?

**TONY.** A plan.

**ZELDA.** He's got a plan!

**RUDY.** *(patting* **TONY** *on the back)* I told you, I told you he knows angles.

**TONY.** It's gonna take some work, kapich?

**JERRY.** Whatever.

**ZELDA.** So, what's the plan?

**TONY.** First off, your brother ain't dead.

**ZELDA.** What!? Isn't dead?

**TONY.** He never died. Yet.

**JERRY.** The man's dead. I looked at him. He has a terrible color.

**TONY.** But who knows?

**SALLY.** The undertaker knows.

**TONY.** So? They make mistakes.

**RUDY.** But the guy embalmed him.

**TONY.** That's his story. Do I know he embalmed, do you know he embalmed? So far as I'm concerned the man was never in a funeral home, he never left his bed.

**ZELDA.** You call this a plan?

**TONY.** The man is alive, but near death's door. This is your story.

**ZELDA.** This is crazy.

**TONY.** You asked for a plan, I'm giving you a plan.

**JERRY.** Maybe we should take a pass on the whole thing.

**SALLY.** And give up getting Louise's silverware?

**TONY.** You wanna hear the rest of the plan, or not? I got no time for fooling around. I gotta fire starting at three-thirty.

**RUDY.** Look, we asked for a plan and he's giving us a plan.

**ZELDA.** Okay, okay.

**SALLY.** What's the rest of the plan?

**TONY.** First off, like I said, the man...what's his name?

**JERRY.** Sam.

**TONY.** Sam ain't dead. Okay? So what we do is move his body into the spare bedroom. Then, I take his place.

**ZELDA.** Nobody can take Sam's place.

**JERRY.** He was a one of a kind.

**SALLY.** They threw away the mold.

**RUDY.** Christ! We've been through this. Let's listen to what the man has to say.

**TONY.** Okay, after we stash him in the spare bedroom, I slip into one of his robes an get in his bed where I am now Sam.

**SALLY.** So you're now Sam, so what?

**TONY.** So now we call in a notary to witness Sam's will.

**ZELDA.** The clouds are now clearing.

**JERRY.** Ah ha!

**SALLY.** So then you dictate a new will giving us the inheritance.

**TONY.** You got it.

**RUDY.** Brilliant!

**SALLY.** Fantastic!

**JERRY.** What a mind!

**ZELDA.** What a plan!

**RUDY.** I told you, the man's a genius.

**TONY.** All right, all right, cut the chatter. We gotta get down to business here. First off I gotta know what each of ya want so's I can tell the notary.

**RUDY.** Right. We'll make a list. *(heading for the desk)*

**JERRY.** I gotta hand it to ya Cappallini, what a scheme.

**ZELDA.** I can't wait to see the look on Father Michaels' face when he sees the new will.

**SALLY.** This is what he gets for preying on a dying person.

**RUDY.** *(returns with a sheet of paper and pen, hands them to **TONY**)* Here ya go.

**TONY.** Okay now, who wants what?

*(And overlapping cacophony breaks out as family members make their demands: townhouse, beach house, stocks, bonds, furniture, jewelry, silverware, linens, paintings, appliances, money, insurance business, real estate, etc. **TONY** has to restore order.)*

Stop it! That's it! Enough already!

*(The family falls silent.)*

Holy Mother in Heaven! One at a time, okay? Now, who goes first?

**RUDY.** I'll go first.

**SALLY.** Where does it say you go first?

**RUDY.** I was his favorite.

**SALLY.** No you weren't. Everybody knows he liked me best.

**ZELDA.** With all due respect, I'm the oldest. I should go first.

**RUDY.** Ahead of your own son?

**JERRY.** What about me, I'm chopped liver?

**ZELDA.** I don't think he liked you.

**JERRY.** Who says?

**ZELDA.** When you came into the room his eyes never lit up.

**SALLY.** His eyes always lit up when he saw me.

**RUDY.** What the hell do eyes lighting up have to do with

anything? Who you think took him for walks in the park with peanuts?

**JERRY.** This was your way of sucking up to him.

**SALLY.** Right. You were just trying to get next to him. Nobody likes to walk in the park with muggers.

**ZELDA.** Who, night after night, read him Tom Clancy? If anybody around here goes first, it should be me.

**JERRY.** I was the only one who could relate to him on a business level. We had conversations.

**RUDY.** About calendars?

**SALLY.** None of you ever had to cancel nail appointments. You have any idea what it's like going around with chipped acrylics?

**TONY.** Hold on! Jesus! You people gotta stop arguing and make a decision.

**RUDY.** Okay… I decide to go first.

**JERRY.** Like hell.

**TONY.** Hey! Stop fighting! We got ground to cover.

**ZELDA.** Tony's right.

**TONY.** Okay…here's the deal…we'll go in alphabetical order.

**JERRY.** Good. This makes sense.

**RUDY.** It makes sense to you because you're a J and I'm an R.

**JERRY.** Can I help it if I'm a J? I was born a J. Okay, I go first.

**TONY.** All right. What's your request?

**JERRY.** I want the insurance business.

**ZELDA.** What!?

**RUDY.** This is a joke.

**SALLY.** It makes sense because he's a businessman.

**ZELDA.** Peddling calendars is a business?

**RUDY.** Sam would want me to have it.

**JERRY.** Who says?

**ZELDA.** Sam probably wanted to turn the business over to a young person. The man was all about the future.

**JERRY.** Who says I'm old?

**SALLY.** Dad's the picture of health. Look at him. He doesn't even own an aspirin.

**RUDY.** But he owns Advil. I've seen him take it.

**TONY.** Hey! We're gettin' nowhere. And we still gotta get a notary. So what's with the business?

**ZELDA.** Okay, give him the business.

**RUDY.** My own mother.

**TONY.** Okay. *(writing as he speaks)* Jerry…gets…the business. Okay, who's next?

**RUDY.** I'm an R…I go next.

**TONY.** So whadaya want, kid?

**RUDY.** Put me down for the townhouse.

**JERRY.** What would you do with a townhouse?

**ZELDA.** Stay out of this. You got the insurance business, didn't you?

**RUDY.** Yeah, what's it to you?

**SALLY.** He's doing this for spite because he knows I want the townhouse.

**RUDY.** You can have the beach house.

**SALLY.** I don't want the beach house. I'm allergic to water.

**ZELDA.** Since when?

**JERRY.** Since always. She can't even go near Perrier.

**TONY.** She doesn't have to live in it. She can sell it.

**ZELDA.** Sam would want us to keep it in the family.

**JERRY.** Sally should get the townhouse.

**RUDY.** You get the insurance business and now Sally wants the townhouse? If she gets the townhouse Jerry can't have the insurance business.

**ZELDA.** Too much would be going to one side of the family.

**SALLY.** What are you talking about? What if you get the stocks and money and Rudy gets the townhouse?

**TONY.** *(impatient with the bickering)* Wait a minute! Wait a minute! What the hell? What am I dealing with here, crazies? Look, from the way I see it, from a very limited perspective, there's plenty for everyone. So you're gonna have to compromise. Like I did when I gave up Manhattan to the Tortellis at the very tragic funeral for Joe Martino.

JERRY. Okay, I'll compromise, except I'm not giving up the insurance business.

RUDY. And I'm willing to bend except for the townhouse.

TONY. This is not my definition of compromise. Look, we gotta settle down here and be reasonable. We'll start over with Jerry. *(from this point the lights begin to dim slowly to black as they bicker)* Jerry, you want the insurance business. Right?

JERRY. Correct.

RUDY. A disgrace. But I'll go along with it.

ZELDA. A million dollar operation to a calendar peddler.

SALLY. It's only fair.

JERRY. I deserve it.

RUDY. The business will be belly-up in six months.

JERRY. Oh, yeah?

RUDY. Yeah.

TONY. I'm putting him down for the business.

SALLY. Good.

ZELDA. Not so fast.

RUDY. *(to* TONY:*)* You're putting down too fast.

JERRY. He's putting down okay.

ZELDA. For you okay, for me too fast.

   *(Lights out.)*


**End of Scene One**

## Act Two, Scene Two

*(An hour later.)*

**TONY.** *(folding a copy of the list and placing it in his inside coat pocket)* Okay. That's that. Now, while we're waiting for the notary, we gotta move the body.

**RUDY.** I went through his pockets, now I gotta move him?

**JERRY.** I'm very superstitious about handling dead people.

**TONY.** You get used to it.

**RUDY.** Maybe we can just cover him up and you can sit in a chair.

**TONY.** It won't work, the man's gotta be on his deathbed.

**ZELDA.** Sick in a chair is not dying.

**TONY.** *(heading for the bedroom)* Okay, let's get at it.

*(The rest of the group follows him into the bedroom.)*

It'll only take a minute.

**SALLY.** I hate dead people.

**ZELDA.** That's no way to talk about your uncle.

**SALLY.** And I'm allergic to embalming fluid.

**RUDY.** Holy crap, Sally, you can't be allergic to everything.

**TONY.** There was no embalming, remember? The man ain't dead.

**SALLY.** It's hard to remember he's alive when he's dead.

**ZELDA.** We can't have any slip-ups when the notary gets here.

**JERRY.** Right. They run around with that little stamp and they think they got authority.

**TONY.** *(at the bed)* Okay, c'mon, gimmie a hand here.

**RUDY.** I don't like it.

**JERRY.** What if we drop him?

**TONY.** He won't feel thing. C'mon. You guys get the head, I'll take the feet.

**JERRY.** How come we get the heavy part?

**TONY.** Can the complaining. Let's get him outta here.

*(RUDY and JERRY take SAM's head, TONY his feet. The lift him from the bed and waddle with him toward the spare bedroom.)*

RUDY. I never realized he was so heavy.

JERRY. You think the man could have dieted.

ZELDA. He never saw a carbohydrate he didn't like.

SALLY. When I went out of my way to visit him from my very busy schedule he was always eating sweets.

TONY. *(As they lug SAM through the doorway to the spare bedroom.)* Easy on your end.

*(The men disappear into the spare bedroom with the body.)*

ZELDA. I hope they don't wrinkle up his only suit.

SALLY. I'm more concerned about Dad's back. It's a fifth lumbar.

ZELDA. You grandfather had the same problem. It stared when be bent over to pick up the cat.

SALLY. This is what happens when people keep pets.

RUDY. *(Emerging from the spare bedroom followed by TONY and JERRY. JERRY is holding his back.)* Okay. That's that.

JERRY. Thank God.

TONY. Now I gotta get into a robe.

ZELDA. There's one in the closet. *(Pointing to the closet.)*

SALLY. It's the one I bought Sam for his birthday, but he never wore it.

TONY. *(opening the closet)* Yeah, looks brand new.

SALLY. See if the tags are on it, maybe I can still take it back.

JERRY. Will it fit?

SALLY. It's a one-size-fits-all.

TONY. *(removing the robe)* It looks good. Here.

*(He takes the will list from his inside pocket, removes his coat and hands them to RUDY. RUDY takes a hanger from the closet, and begins to hang TONY's coat on it.)*

RUDY. *(noting the coat.)* Nice coat.

TONY. *(slipping into the robe)* I had it made for a memorial service for a good friend who tripped and fell off a building in the Bronx. *(in the robe)* Perfect fit.

(**RUDY** *hangs the coat in the closet and hands the will list to* **TONY**.)

SALLY. Now what?

RUDY. Now he gets into the bed where he's dying.

TONY. Right. I get in the bed and wait for the notary.

ZELDA. If you get bored, there's a magazine with questionable content on the nightstand.

**End of Scene Two**

## Act Two, Scene Three

*(A bit later. The family is in the living room.* TONY *is sitting up in bed in the dimly-lit bedroom.)*

JERRY. Does he look sick? He doesn't look sick.

ZELDA. What you expect? The man's only been dead for ten minutes.

SALLY. He's too healthy to be dying.

RUDY. A person can look like a million bucks and have a heart attack the next second.

ZELDA. He doesn't look a thing like Sam.

RUDY. So what? What will the notary know?

JERRY. What if she's suspicious?

RUDY. Why would she be suspicious?

SALLY. Because he looks too good. A Sun-tanned Italian. It'll be like taking a will from Dean Martin.

ZELDA. Let's not get paranoid. What can go wrong?

RUDY. She'll come in, do the will and be history.

SALLY. What if she has to testify.

RUDY. So she testifies to taking a will from a Sam Price. At this point Sam will be underground. Who's she gonna identify through six feet of dirt?

JERRY. This is what we get for getting mixed up with a Cappallini.

RUDY. It's too late. We all agreed.

ZELDA. He may be a person of dubious extraction, but the man's a thinker.

SALLY. We don't know anything about this notary.

RUDY. What's to know? A notary's a notary.

JERRY. Maybe we should have gotten a referral.

ZELDA. A referral could know Sam.

RUDY. We got a referral though the Yellow Pages. This way there's no connection.

SALLY. What if she can't spell?

RUDY. All I care about is that she knows how to spell townhouse.

**SALLY.** This is a very self-centered attitude.

**JERRY.** No bickering.

**ZELDA.** Thanks to Tony we're all gonna be well off, so let's not be at each other's throats.

*(The doorbell sounds.)*

There she is.

**SALLY.** Let's not let on that we're crooks.

**RUDY.** *(heading for the entrance hall)* I'll get it.

*(He disappears into the hallway. His voice is offstage.)*

Hello, I'm Rudy; I spoke with you on he phone, Ms....

**MILDRED.** *(offstage)* Mildred. Mildred Longnecker.

**RUDY.** *(offstage)* Hi, I'm Rudy. Come on in.

*(Entering from the entrance hallway followed by MIL-DRED, a dowdy, shy woman in her mid-fifties. She is carrying a briefcase. RUDY makes introductions.)*

Mildred, I'd like you to meet my mother, Zelda; my uncle, Jerry; and my cousin, Sally.

**MILDRED.** Glad to meet you.

**ZELDA.** We're so glad you could come on such short notice.

**MILDRED.** It's been a slow notary day.

**SALLY.** Do you get called out often?

**MILDRED.** Every now and then. Mostly I work in the office.

**JERRY.** We have a very sick man here, Mildred.

**MILDRED.** You do? Where?

**RUDY.** In the bedroom.

**SALLY.** Even though he may not look it.

**ZELDA.** He was athletic, and athletes even look good when they're terminally ill.

**JERRY.** He needs you to hear his will.

**MILDRED.** I see. I hope the poor man won't be too weak.

**RUDY.** Oh no. No no!

**SALLY.** Even though he may be weak, his faculties are still in tact.

**ZELDA.** He's only lost control over his reading material.

MILDRED. I've had lots of deathbed clients. All ages.

SALLY. Interesting.

MILDRED. They call me in for last minute changes. For strange requests. Last week I got called in for a woman who was dying from a car accident. She left everything to her insurance adjuster.

JERRY. Are you fully licensed?

MILDRED. Yes.

RUDY. We wanna be sure this is official.

MILDRED. *(digging into her briefcase)* Just a moment, I'll show you my certificate.

*(She digs into her briefcase and withdraws the document, hands it to* RUDY.*)*

Here. Just renewed in April.

RUDY. Looks good. *(hands it to* JERRY*)*

JERRY. Yes. *(hands it to* ZELDA*)*

ZELDA. Yes. *(passes it to* SALLY*)*

SALLY. *(immediately handing it back to* MILDRED*)* Here. I'm allergic to red tape.

RUDY. Okay, we'll take you in to meet the deceased… *(quickly covering up)* almost deceased!

*(He leads the way into the bedroom followed by the others.* MILDRED *squints into the gloom.)*

MILDRED. Kind of dark, isn't it?

JERRY. We like to keep the lights down.

SALLY. Out of respect.

RUDY. *(calling to* TONY*)* Uncle Sam. *(no response)* Uncle Sam, someone's here to see you.

TONY. *(weakly)* Someone…? To see me…?

ZELDA. Yes, Sam.

SALLY. Someone with a legitimate certificate.

TONY. *(weakly)* Who…who is it…?

RUDY. It's the notary public like you requested.

TONY. *(weakly)* A nosy Republican?

**ZELDA.** Notary! Notary public!

**TONY.** Oh...yes...notary public.

**SALLY.** She's come to listen to you make your will.

**TONY.** Bring her over. Bring her over closer.

*(They approach the bed slowly.)*

**MILDRED.** He doesn't look sick.

**SALLY.** What are you talking about? The man's the picture of death.

**ZELDA.** As they say, the bulb always burns brighter before it blows out.

**SALLY.** As they say.

**TONY.** What's your name, dear?

**MILDRED.** Mildred.

**TONY.** Come closer Mildred, let me have a look at you. *(MILDRED moves in closer and TONY squints at her.)* Yes... you look exactly like a notary public. Pull up a chair, honey. And please hurry. I'm fading fast.

*(He emits a weak cough. MILDRED goes to a chair and pulls it close to the bed.)*

**RUDY.** We'll leave you alone.

**ZELDA.** Yes, we don't wanna disrupt the will.

**JERRY.** Call us if you need anything.

*(The family leaves the room and takes seats in the living room. MILDRED opens her briefcase and withdraws papers and a seal.)*

**TONY.** *(coughs, clears his throat)* Okay. Are you ready?

**MILDRED.** Yes.

**TONY.** *(as the lights goes down on both rooms)* Okay...I, Samuel Price, being of sound mind, hereby...

*(Lights out.)*

**End of Scene Three**

## Act Two, Scene Four

*(One hour later.)*

*(The family is sitting silently in the living room.* **TONY** *hops from the bed, goes to the closet, removes the robe and hangs it in the closet, takes his suit coat from he closet and puts it on. He goes to the nightstand and gets copies of the will, one of which he folds neatly and places in his inside coat pocket. He enters the living room, carrying a copy of the will, which he hands to* **ZELDA***:)*

**TONY.** Here ya go. Notarized and sealed.

**ZELDA.** *(taking the will)* Thank you.

**SALLY.** We'll be eternally grateful to the grave.

**RUDY.** It was a beautiful plan.

**TONY.** Not bad. Now you gotta get Sam man back in bed. Do you need a hand?

**JERRY.** Rudy and I can manage.

**TONY.** You sure?

**RUDY.** Yeah. No problem.

**TONY.** Well then, I gotta get the hell outta here. I got commitments in Jersey.

**ZELDA.** This is a special favor that we won't soon forget.

**TONY.** *(patting* **RUDY** *on the cheek)* I did it for this beautiful boy who I love like a son. Okay...gotta go. See ya in church.

*(He exits quickly.)*

**SALLY.** A wonderful man

**ZELDA.** The man has class.

**JERRY.** You could tell by the suit.

**SALLY.** He was sweet and considerate.

**ZELDA.** As they say, you can't believe what you read in the papers.

**SALLY.** As they say.

**RUDY.** I called. He came over. How many people would go out of their way?

**JERRY.** Whatta guy. Because of him I'm now in the insurance business.

**ZELDA.** *(holding up the will)* Here it is.

**SALLY.** Notarized and sealed.

**ZELDA.** *(begins to read the will)* "I, Samuel Price, being of sound mind, hereby bequeath to following to…"

*(She reads on for a few seconds then suddenly displays great shock.)*

Jesus! Why that dirty, double-crossing sonofabitch!

**RUDY.** What is it!?

**JERRY.** What's wrong!?

**ZELDA.** I can't believe this!

**SALLY.** What the hell is it!?

**RUDY.** *(jerking the will away from ZELDA)* Gimmie that!

*(He peruses the will.)*

Holy crap! Holy crap! Holy crap!

**JERRY.** Will ya quit with the "Holy craps," for crisesakes. What the hell is it!?

**RUDY.** *(handing the will to JERRY)* He left everything to himself!

**SALLY.** What!?

**JERRY.** *(looking at the will)* He gets it all. The man's a devil.

**ZELDA.** He set us up. Took advantage of us.

**SALLY.** I can't believe this.

**JERRY.** Believe it, it's in their blood.

**RUDY.** And he said he loved me like a son.

**ZELDA.** We shoulda known better than to trust the dishonest SOB.

**SALLY.** He and Michaels, two of a kind .

**ZELDA.** Of all the rotten, goddamned…

**JERRY.** Dirty bastard!

**RUDY.** *(jerking the will from JERRY)* Let me take another look at that thing. *(He scans the will.)*

**ZELDA.** It's all there, in black and white.

**JERRY.** Sealed and notarized.

**SALLY.** This means I'll wind up working for a living.

**RUDY.** *(staring at the will)* Wait a minute! Hold on!

**ZELDA.** What!?

**RUDY.** There's a clause.

**JERRY.** Of course there's a clause. There's always a clause.

**RUDY.** *(pointing at the will)* Here…here at the end.

**ZELDA.** So there's a clause. So we're still screwed.

**RUDY.** Maybe not.

**SALLY.** Whadaya mean, maybe not?

**RUDY.** Get this. If Doris and I get married, everything goes back to the family as requested.

**JERRY.** You're kidding?

**ZELDA.** *(snatching the will)* Lemme see that! *(looking at the will)* I'll be damned.

**JERRY.** If you marry his daughter, I'm back in the insurance business?

**ZELDA.** *(looking at the will)* That's what it says.

**SALLY.** All you have to do it marry the big hair?

**RUDY.** Yep. That's all.

**JERRY.** *(grabbing **RUDY**'s hand enthusiastically)* Well…you have my blessing.

**RUDY.** This is beautiful. What a guy.

**SALLY.** I guess she isn't that bad. She can always get a normal hairdo.

**ZELDA.** Even though I'm not a hundred percent, I can live with it.

**JERRY.** *(pumping **RUDY**'s hand)* Congratulations on a wonderful engagement.

**ZELDA.** It'll be nice welcoming her into the family.

**JERRY.** Wonderful girl, wonderful girl. What's her name again?

**RUDY.** Doris.

**JERRY.** Doris, of course – Doris.

**SALLY.** I'll meet her some day for pizza.

**RUDY.** Once you get to know her, you'll see why I love her.

**JERRY.** We can't wait to meet her.

**ZELDA.** Looking back, I can see now that I was maybe viewing things from a jaded perspective.

**SALLY.** Do you think they'll serve lasagna at the reception?

*(Lights down on the living room and a spot up on TONY downstage left.)*

**TONY.** *(Takes the copy of the will from his pocket, unfolds it, and scans it. Looks up at the audience.)* Well...maybe it was underhanded, ya know. But for love, it was worth it.

### Curtain

**Also by**
# Roger Karshner...

**Clothes Encounters**

**Don't Say Goodbye, I'm Not Leaving**

**The Dream Crust**

**Hot Turkey at Midnight**

**Love on the Cusp**

**The Man with the Plastic Sandwich**

**Monkey's Uncle**

**To Live at the Pitch**

Please visit our website **samuelfrench.com** for complete
descriptions and licensing information

# OTHER TITLES AVAILABLE FROM SAMUEL FRENCH

## THE OFFICE PLAYS
Two full length plays by Adam Bock

### THE RECEPTIONIST
*Comedy / 2m., 2f. Interior*

At the start of a typical day in the Northeast Office, Beverly deals effortlessly with ringing phones and her colleague's romantic troubles. But the appearance of a charming rep from the Central Office disrupts the friendly routine. And as the true nature of the company's business becomes apparent, The Receptionist raises disquieting, provocative questions about the consequences of complicity with evil.

"...Mr. Bock's poisoned Post-it note of a play." - *New York Times*

"Bock's intense initial focus on the routine goes to the heart of *The Receptionist's* pointed, painfully timely allegory... elliptical, provocative play..."
- *Time Out New York*

### THE THUGS
*Comedy / 2m, 6f / Interior*

The Obie Award winning dark comedy about work, thunder and the mysterious things that are happening on the 9th floor of a big law firm. When a group of temps try to discover the secrets that lurk in the hidden crevices of their workplace, they realize they would rather believe in gossip and rumors than face dangerous realities.

"Bock starts you off giggling, but leaves you with a chill."
- *Time Out New York*

"... a delightfully paranoid little nightmare that is both more chillingly realistic and pointedly absurd than anything John Grisham ever dreamed up."
- *New York Times*

SAMUELFRENCH.COM

CPSIA information can be obtained at www.ICGtesting.com
Printed in the USA
LVOW081634090713

342073LV00018B/731/P